www.raintreepublishers.co.uk
Visit our website to find out
more information about
Raintree books.

To order:
☎ Phone 0845 6044371
▤ Fax +44 (0) 1865 312263
▣ Email myorders@raintreepublishers.co.uk

Customers from outside the UK please telephone +44 1865 312262

Raintree is an imprint of Capstone Global Library Limited,
a company incorporated in England and Wales having its registered office at 7 Pilgrim
Street, London, EC4V 6LB
– Registered company number: 6695582

Art Director: Bob Lentz
Designer: Hilary Wacholz
Production Specialist: Michelle Biedschied
Editor: Catherine Veitch
Originated by Capstone Global Library Ltd
Printed and bound in China by Leo Paper Products Ltd

ISBN 978 1 406 22659 1 (paperback)
15 14 13 12 11
10 9 8 7 6 5 4 3 2 1

British Library Cataloguing in Publication Data
A full catalogue record for this book is available
from the British Library.

The story of *The Elves and the Shoemaker* has been passed down for generations. There are many versions of the story. The following tale is a retelling of the original version. While the story has been cut for length and level, the basic elements of the classic tale remain.

The characters

Read the story to meet these characters and find out who they are ...

There once was a poor shoemaker. He could buy only enough leather to make one pair of shoes at a time.

One night, he cut the leather for the
shoes he wanted to make the next day.
Then he went to bed.

The next morning, a pair of shoes was already made! The shoes were perfect.

A rich man paid twice the price for them.
The shoemaker was able to buy enough
leather for two pairs of shoes.

Again, he cut the leather for the shoes
he planned to make the next day.

The next morning, two pairs of shoes were made. These shoes sold right away, too. The shoemaker made enough money to buy leather for four pairs of shoes.

The next morning, four pairs of shoes were made. And so it went on.

The shoemaker made a lot of money.
Before long, he was rich.

One night, he said to his wife,
"Let's stay up tonight. Maybe we can
see who is helping us."

That night, the shoemaker and his
wife hid.

Around midnight, two naked little men sat down at the table. They worked all night.

The shoemaker and his wife watched.

When the shoes were done, the little men ran away.

"Those two little men have made us rich. We should help them," the wife said.

"What should we do?" asked the shoemaker.

"Well, they don't have any clothes," his wife said. "I will make them coats, shirts, trousers, and socks."

"And I will make them shoes," the shoemaker said.

The shoemaker and his wife waited for Christmas Eve. Then they put the shoes and the clothes on the table.

Around midnight, the little men showed up again.

They saw the shoes and the clothes.

They were very surprised.

They quickly put the clothes on.
Then they started to sing.

"Now we are men so fine to see," they sang.
"No longer shoemakers shall we be."

The little men danced and danced.

At last, they danced out of the door.
And they were never seen again.

The shoemaker and his wife were rewarded for their good deeds. They succeeded in everything they tried. And they lived happily ever after.

The End